THE • COBBLE • STREET • COUSINS

IN
AUNT LUCY'S
KITCHEN

A LITTLE SHOPPING

CYNTHIA RYLANT

illustrated by

WENDY ANDERSON HALPERIN

Aladdin Paperbacks
NEW YORK   LONDON   TORONTO   SYDNEY

First Aladdin Paperbacks edition June 2004

The Cobble Street Cousins: In Aunt Lucy's Kitchen text copyright © 1998
by Cynthia Rylant
The Cobble Street Cousins: In Aunt Lucy's Kitchen illustrations copyright © 1998
by Wendy Anderson Halperin
The Cobble Street Cousins: A Little Shopping text copyright © 1998 by
Cynthia Rylant
The Cobble Street Cousins: A Little Shopping illustrations copyright © 1998
by Wendy Anderson Halperin

ALADDIN PAPERBACKS
An imprint of Simon & Schuster Children's Publishing Division
1230 Avenue of the Americas, New York, NY 10020

These titles are also available individually in **SIMON & SCHUSTER BOOKS
FOR YOUNG READERS** hardcover editions.

The text of this book was set in Garth Graphic.

Printed in the United States of America
2 4 6 8 10 9 7 5 3 1

CIP Data for these titles is available from the Library of Congress.

Library of Congress Control Number:
The Cobble Hill Cousins: In Aunt Lucy's Kitchen 97-20995
The Cobble Hill Cousins: A Little Shopping 97-20996

ISBN 0-689-87103-1

THE • COBBLE • STREET • COUSINS

IN
AUNT LUCY'S
KITCHEN

CYNTHIA RYLANT

illustrated by

WENDY ANDERSON HALPERIN

ALADDIN PAPERBACKS
New York London Toronto Sydney Singapore

TABLE OF
CONTENTS

For Cousin Jenn

C.R.

For Cousins Mare, Lane, and Molly

W.A.H.

IN
AUNT LUCY'S
KITCHEN

THE
COOKIE COMPANY

On Cobble Street in a light blue house with pretty pink curtains and geraniums by the door, there lived three girl cousins and their aunt named Lucy.

The cousins were Lily, Rosie, and Tess, and they were all nine years old. They were living with Aunt Lucy for a year because their parents—all of whom were dancers—

1

were touring the world with the ballet, and the three girls knew that they did not want to go to boarding school and they did not want to live in hotels all the time. They wanted to play and to live in a house.

So they lived with Aunt Lucy.

Aunt Lucy was wonderful. She owned a flower shop on the corner and every day she went to her little shop and sold flowers to all the people in the neighborhood. Even people who did not like flowers very much bought Aunt Lucy's flowers, for she was so friendly and so pretty—with her long red hair and colorful dresses— and her shop was so inviting. She even made tea for her customers.

Lily, Rosie, and Tess shared a bedroom in the attic of Aunt Lucy's house. It was a very large attic (for the house itself was large and very old and, of course, a bit drafty in winter), and each girl had her own "room" within the attic.

Lily's room, in the middle of the attic, was surrounded by long, lacy yellow curtains. Inside her curtained room she had a small wicker bed, a trunk all painted with roses (for her rabbit collection), and a small table for writing. Lily liked to write poems.

Rosie (who was Lily's sister) made her
room in the south corner of the attic, near the
stained-glass window which Rosie loved so
well. She loved the colors of the glass spread-
ing all around her on sunny days. Rosie's bed
was tucked behind an old patchwork quilt,
and on her bed she kept her rag doll, Angel
Girl, and her bear, Henry. And in a pretty blue
suitcase beside the bed was Rosie's collection
of paper dolls.

Tess's room was at the other end of the
attic, behind a large screen painted with palm
trees (from Aunt Lucy's trip to Hawaii). Tess
loved music, and she had a small record player
beside her bed which had been her father's
when he was a boy. Tess kept a large stack of
old records in a milk crate, and she played
them all the time. She knew all the words to
the old songs. When she grew up, Tess wanted
to be on Broadway.

Tess also had a cat, which Aunt Lucy kindly let her keep. The cat's name was Elliott and he was black and white and slept on Tess's bed most of the day. The cousins all loved him. And Aunt Lucy brought catnip from her flower shop every afternoon.

The girls had moved into Aunt Lucy's attic in June, and now they had the whole summer ahead of them. Naturally they were considering what summer things they might do, and it was Lily who came up with the idea of a cookie company.

"A cookie company?" asked Tess, as the three sat dangling their legs on Aunt Lucy's front porch swing.

"Sure," said Lily. "Everybody loves cookies. We could take orders from the neighbors and deliver fresh-baked cookies right to their doors."

"Yum," said Rosie. She was holding her favorite paper doll, a Victorian girl dressed all in white with a dog in her arms.

"How do we advertise?" asked Tess.

"Lily could write a poem," said Rosie.

"Good idea!" said Tess.

Lily nodded her head.

"I could do that," she said.

"We could put the ad in Aunt Lucy's shop. And in French's Market," said Rosie.

"And on the library bulletin board," said Tess.

"Do you think Aunt Lucy will let us?" asked Rosie.

"For free cookies? Sure!" said Lily.

Lily was right. Aunt Lucy agreed to let the girls have a cookie company.

"Remember, clean hands—clean kitchen," said Aunt Lucy. "And aprons for everyone."

"We promise," said the cousins.

"I especially love Cinnamon Crinkles," said Aunt Lucy with a smile.

So Cinnamon Crinkles were the first cookies the girls baked. And they were delicious! Even Elliott thought so, for he ate up all the little pieces of dough left under the kitchen table.

"We're ready to advertise," said Lily.

She made up a poem and Tess and Rosie printed the posters:

The cousins were in business!

DELIVERIES

$\mathcal{A}$ few days later, the Cobble Street Cookie Company received its first order.

Rosie answered the phone.

"Hello, is this the cookie company?" asked a woman's voice.

"Yes it is!" said Rosie excitedly. "May we help you?"

The woman asked Rosie to deliver one dozen fresh-baked Cinnamon Crinkles to her apartment on Friday. Her book club was having a meeting.

Rosie took the order, hung up the phone, and nearly fainted with delight!

Just then the phone rang again. Someone was having a birthday party. Could the company deliver some cookies?

Soon after that, the phone rang *again*. Someone was home from the hospital. Could the company make some cookies, please?

Rosie wrote down the orders as fast as she could. When finally the phone stopped ringing, she called to the girls.

"Lily! Tess! We have customers!"

The next day the cousins put on their aprons and baked all morning long. Lily was in charge of pouring the ingredients, Rosie was in charge of mixing, Tess rolled up the little balls of dough.

While the cookies baked, the girls dreamed of what they would do if the cookie company made them rich.

"I'm going to move to New York," said Tess. "I'll live in a penthouse and go to Broadway musicals every single day. And I'll have an Irish setter."

"I'd like a little cottage," said Rosie. "With flowers and a fish pond and lots of stained glass."

"I'm going to travel," said Lily. "To China or India or Africa. I'll wear flowing scarves and carry a canary and ride on trains."

Ding-ding.

"Cookies are ready!" everyone cried.

By afternoon, the cousins had four dozen cookies made and ready to deliver. They put on fresh dresses, tucked bows in their hair, and kissed Elliott good-bye.

Their first stop was the brick apartment building two blocks over on Vine Street. It was a wonderful old building with stone lions guarding the front and topiary trees.

"I'll bet there's some stained glass in this

building," said Rosie as the girls rang the buzzer for Apartment 5.

A woman's voice answered.

"Yes?"

"Cookie Company!" said Tess loudly. Lily giggled. Tess was so *professional*!

"Come right in," said the woman, and she buzzed the girls through the entry door.

The hallway floors were marble, and a beautiful fountain with cherubs stood just inside the door.

"Wow," said Rosie, letting the water splash on her fingers.

The girls smoothed down their hair and checked each other's bows, then knocked on the door of Apartment 5.

Presently the door opened and a very tall woman in a suit and high heels smiled at them. She had large gold earrings and very red lipstick.

"Wonderful!" she said. "Do come in."

The cousins stepped into Apartment 5. They passed through a narrow foyer, then out into the living room.

"Wow," said Rosie again.

The living room really was a *living* room, for it was filled with enormous indoor plants. Tall tropical trees raised their giant leaves to the ceiling. Vines trailed across windowsills. Cacti bloomed with scarlet flowers. There were even orchids growing on a window seat.

On one of the sofas sat a young man with his leg in a cast. He was thin and looked tired about the eyes, but he gave the girls a sweet smile.

"Cinnamon Crinkles," he said. "After two weeks of hospital food, they're just what I need."

The cousins smiled. None of the girls knew what to say, even Tess. They were all so impressed by everything.

"This is my brother, Michael," said the woman in the suit.

"How do you do," said Lily with a curtsy. Rosie stared at Lily. Where did Lily learn to do *that*?

Tess found her voice.

"I'm Tess, this is Rosie, and that's her sister, Lily. We're cousins and we live with our Aunt Lucy on Cobble Street."

The woman and her brother smiled at the girls.

"How nice to live with one's cousins," said the woman.

"Yes," said Rosie. "We have rooms in the attic. My room has stained glass."

"Oh, I love stained glass," said the woman. "We have a lovely stained-glass window in the kitchen."

"You do?" Rosie said excitedly.

"Yes," said the woman. "You can bring the cookies in the kitchen and while I get my purse, you can admire the glass."

"Oh, good!" said Rosie.

"By the way, my name is Mrs. Haverstock," said the woman as she and Rosie walked toward the hallway.

Lily and Tess stood shyly in the living room, their eyes following the trees to the ceiling.

"The ceilings in this building are fifteen feet tall," said Michael. "I'm thinking of installing a giraffe to go with my trees."

The girls giggled.

"How did you break your leg?" asked Tess. Lily nudged her in the side for her bad manners. Lily had been taught never to ask personal questions. But Tess was so out-going, she asked everyone everything.

"I am embarrassed to say that I fell off a ledge," said Michael.

"Really?" said Tess, who was a bit clumsy herself and glad to meet another stumbler.

"Yes, believe it or not, it was at the art museum," said Michael. "I climbed onto the ledge alongside the stairs in front of the building, to see what was in a nest, and I got so interested in what I was doing, I fell off."

"I do that all the time," said Tess.

Michael smiled.

"What was in the nest?" asked Lily.

"Baby birds," said Michael. "Swallows, I think."

Tess looked all around at the trees and plants.

"Aunt Lucy would love this place," she said.

"She enjoys plants?" asked Michael.

"*Loves* them," said Tess. "She owns Lucy's Flowers on the corner of Cobble and Plum."

"*That's* your Aunt Lucy?" asked Michael.

"Yes," Lily and Tess answered together.

"Do you know her?" asked Tess.

"Oh . . ." Michael hesitated. "Not really. No. I just . . . I was in a few times and . . . noticed her."

Lily and Tess glanced at each other. Michael was *blushing*!

"You should stop in the shop for tea sometime," said Tess. "Tell Aunt Lucy that we sent you."

Michael smiled.

"Well, as soon as I'm able to hobble about, perhaps I will."

Rosie and Mrs. Haverstock returned to the living room. Rosie was all smiles.

"You should see the stained glass," she said.

"We'd like to, but we have to go," said Lily. "We have one more delivery to make."

"Well, thank you so very much," said Mrs. Haverstock. "You girls are delightful."

The cousins grinned. What a good time they were having!

"Michael, don't forget Aunt Lucy!" said Tess. This time, *Lily* was blushing—at Tess's boldness.

Michael smiled.

"I won't," he said. "Good-bye for now."

Outside on the sidewalk the girls were all chatter.

"He likes Aunt Lucy!" said Tess.

"I know! I know!" said Lily. "He turned so pink!"

"What are you talking about?" said Rosie.

And on their way to the next delivery, Lily and Tess told Rosie all about Michael.

"He fell off a ledge?" asked Rosie, ever practical. "How could he fall off a ledge?"

"He's in love with Aunt Lucy and all you can wonder is how he fell off a ledge?" asked Tess dramatically.

"He should write a poem for Aunt Lucy," said Lily. "I could help him."

"Here's the house," said Tess, back to business. The girls checked the address. Yes, it was the house with the birthday party. But it seemed rather quiet for a birthday. There were no cars parked in front. No balloons on the door. Just a small pink house with organdy curtains and an umbrella by the front door.

The girls walked onto the porch and rang the bell.

They waited and waited and waited, and just as Tess was about to ring again, the front door slowly opened.

And there stood a very old woman. She was rather hunched and very frail, but she had beautiful white hair and sparkling blue eyes.

"Ah," she said sweetly, "birthday cookies. Please come in."

The cousins quietly and politely stepped inside the door. The house was dark and silent and smelled faintly of lavender.

"I am Mrs. White," said the elderly woman, shaking hands with each girl. "Please come in and sit down while I get your money."

While the cousins walked over to a long

velvet sofa in the living room, Tess introduced herself and Lily and Rosie. They waited as Mrs. White searched in a drawer for her coin purse.

"Whose birthday is it?" asked Tess. Lily nudged her in the side.

Mrs. White, purse in hand, turned to Tess and smiled.

"Why, it's mine, dear," she answered. "I am ninety years old today."

The cousins gasped.

"Ninety years old!" cried Lily. "Oh my goodness!"

"Yes." Mrs. White sat down in a wing chair and smiled at the girls.

"Are you having a big party?" asked Tess. Lily nudged her again.

"Oh no, dear," said Mrs. White. "Just myself. My only son passed away last year. And, well, at ninety, it's rather difficult to make new friends." She smiled. "I don't travel far these days."

Rosie, who had the most tender heart, said at once, "Then we will sing you 'Happy Birthday.' Would that be all right?"

"I'm a *very* good singer," added Tess.

Mrs. White smiled shyly.

"That would be lovely," she said softly.

The cousins stood up, smoothed their dresses, and sang.

When they were finished Mrs. White had tears in her eyes. She applauded them.

"Beautiful," she said. "And Tess, your voice *is* very good."

Tess beamed.

Mrs. White counted out three dollars in coins for the girls.

"Thank you very much for the birthday cookies," she said, handing them the money.

"They're free," blurted Rosie. Lily and Tess looked at her in surprise.

"Oh no, dear, please, I do want to pay for them," said Mrs. White.

"No, no," said Rosie sincerely, her eyes wide. "Please let us give them to you for your ninetieth birthday. We've never known anyone who was ninety. Please let us."

Mrs. White looked at Rosie's pleading face. She smiled and put the coins on the table.

"All right, my dear," she said. "But you must let me give each of you one of my little cats."

"Cats?" said Tess. "Oh, we couldn't, Aunt Lucy said only one cat at home and . . . "

"Not real cats, dear," said Mrs. White. "I'll show you."

And she opened a brown wicker sewing basket beside her chair and took out a small cotton cat. It was white with little black eyes, pink whiskers, and a glittery collar.

"I love it!" cried Lily. "I have a rabbit collection," she told Mrs. White.

Mrs. White let each cousin choose the cat she most liked, and then it was time to go.

"Happy birthday, Mrs. White," said Rosie. "We hope you like the Cinnamon Crinkles."

"Thank you so much, my dears. What a lovely day you've given me," said Mrs. White, clasping each girl's hands.

"Bye!" called the cousins as they walked down the sidewalk.

Mrs. White waved to them until they turned the corner and were out of sight.

"I can't wait to tell Aunt Lucy about this day!" cried Tess.

"Me too!" said her cousins.

And they ran all the way home to bake cookies for their Friday delivery.

THE SHOW

The Cobble Street Cookie Company lasted exactly three weeks, and then it folded. Lily, Rosie, and Tess made ten dollars apiece—enough for a new rabbit for Lily, a tea set for Rosie, and

a record for Tess. Then they took down all of the ads, for the girls were quite tired of baking and ready for something new.

"We should go visit Michael," said Lily one afternoon.

"Oh no, Lily," said Rosie. "Mother would never want us intruding."

"But he hasn't come to the shop to see Aunt Lucy yet," said Lily. "He needs a nudge."

"If you nudge him too hard, he might break his other leg," said Tess with a giggle.

"He might fall off a porch," said Rosie.

Tess and Rosie couldn't stop giggling.

"You two are so unromantic!" complained Lily. "We should *do* something!"

The cousins thought about how they might introduce Michael to Aunt Lucy.

39

"Why not have a performance and invite Michael and Mrs. Haverstock?" said Tess.

"What sort of performance?" asked Lily.

"A program," said Tess. "With poetry and song. Like the artists in Paris do."

"I could write a poem to read aloud," said Lily. "Maybe a poem about young lovers finding each other."

"Or falling off a bus," giggled Rosie.

"I could sing, of course," said Tess.

"Something old and romantic, sort of bluesy."

"What shall I do?" asked Rosie.

"Give a lecture on stained glass?" said Lily.

"*No.*" Rosie grinned, giving Lily a little push.

"You could be the host," said Tess. "You can welcome everyone and introduce us, like the Oscars."

"Okay," said Rosie.

"Let's find some paper and make invitations," said Lily.

The girls printed out four decorated invitations: one for Aunt Lucy, one for Michael and Mrs. Haverstock, one for Mrs. White (to be polite, for they doubted she would come), and one for Mr. French of French's Market. He was always so kind to the cousins and had

even given them two free jars of cinnamon when they were in business.

The program was scheduled for Sunday afternoon. It was called "A Collection of Classics by Comely Cousins." (It was Lily's idea. Tess wanted to call it simply "The Show," but Rosie sided with Lily.)

Aunt Lucy was very sweet in helping the girls prepare the house for company. She put pots of daisies and daylilies all around the parlor and made fresh blueberry muffins to serve with tea. She even lit candles and lined them up on the fireplace mantel.

"So *dramatic!*" said Tess.

The cousins weren't sure if anyone would come to the Collection of Classics, but at 1:45 they saw a large green car pull up in front of Aunt Lucy's house.

"It's Mrs. Haverstock!" cried Lily. "And Michael!"

The girls ran outside to greet them. Mrs. Haverstock was all dressed up and smelled of perfume. She looked very elegant, and she smiled broadly at the cousins.

"Hello again!" she called.

Michael pulled himself out of the car and

leaned on a cane. He was dressed more simply, in jeans and a sport coat. He waved shyly at the girls.

Rosie stepped up and shook Michael's hand as the other girls led Mrs. Haverstock into the house.

"Hi, Michael," Rosie said with a big smile. "How are your trees?"

"Taller," said Michael. "Just like you, Rosie. I believe you've grown."

Rosie shook her head and lifted a foot.

"Heels," she whispered. "Tess insisted."

Michael grinned, gave Rosie his arm, and walked her to the front door.

Just inside, Aunt Lucy was helping Mrs. Haverstock with her purse and jacket. Rosie glanced at Michael.

He was blushing again!

Rosie led him proudly to Aunt Lucy.

"This is my Aunt Lucy," said Rosie.

"How are you," said Michael, extending his hand. "I'm Michael Livingston."

45

Even his ears were red! Rosie couldn't wait to tell Lily and Tess, who were busy preparing to perform.

"Hello, Michael," said Aunt Lucy. "The girls are so happy you've come. Would you care to sit down?"

Michael looked at Aunt Lucy's old-fashioned parlor with its wicker rocking chair, its fainting couch, its old family portraits on the wall.

"I love old houses," said Michael.

"Oh, please let me give you a tour," said Aunt Lucy. "We'll be right back, Rosie."

Rosie wanted to scream as they walked away, she was so excited!

Mrs. Haverstock was in the parlor talking with Mr. French, who had just arrived. They knew each other well, for they had gone to high school together many years before. Already they were trading stories and laughing.

Aunt Lucy returned with Michael—she looked so happy!—then just as everyone was seated and Rosie was about to begin her welcome, the doorbell rang.

On the front porch was Mrs. White, holding the arm of a taxi driver.

"Mrs. White!" the three cousins called in delight. Aunt Lucy followed them to welcome Mrs. White into the house.

"I haven't seen a good show in fifty years, my dears," said Mrs. White. "I thought I'd better not miss this one."

"We're so glad you could come, Mrs. White," said Aunt Lucy. "I'm Lucy Weatherbee and, of course, you know my girls."

"Your angels," said Mrs. White with a smile. She thanked the taxi driver and followed everyone to the parlor. Michael and Mr. French both stood up and offered Mrs. White their seats.

"Thank you, gentlemen, but this small chair will do just fine," she said.

Eventually all were introduced and settled and the program began.

Rosie welcomed everyone and wished them

all a happy afternoon. Then she introduced Lily and added, "She will one day be a famous writer and you will be glad you saw her here."

Lily stepped forward and read a long poem about a young woman who was lost at sea.

The poem was at first very sad, and Rosie—always the tender heart—got worried and thought she might cry. But then the young woman was found by her true love and all turned out happily. When it was time for applause, Rosie clapped hardest.

Then she introduced Tess, "one of the finest young singers this side of Broadway," said Rosie. "She will perform, especially for Aunt Lucy, a love song called 'That Sweet New Face.'"

All three girls looked at Michael: red as a strawberry!

Tess, wearing a large purple hat with feathers, stepped into the middle of the room. She took a small harmonica from her pocket, blew a few chords, then began singing. It was such a catchy tune that soon everyone in the room was tapping his feet. Mr. French had a wide

grin on his face and Mrs. Haverstock swayed
back and forth to the rhythm.

At the end of the song, Tess gave a deep
bow to the applause.

Rosie concluded the program by reminding everyone that tea and blueberry muffins would be served. Then all three cousins lined up and said "thank you and good night" in unison. Everyone applauded again.

It was a lovely afternoon. Mrs. White stayed long enough for tea but left before the others did (the same taxi driver came to pick her up). She gave each girl another little cat before she left.

Michael and Mrs. Haverstock and Mr. French and Aunt Lucy all moved into Aunt Lucy's kitchen, where they gathered around the big table and talked and talked. Lily, Rosie, and Tess—who were all ready to get out of the house and play—peeked in at them one last time.

"Aunt Lucy likes Michael, I can tell," said Lily.

"Just think, it all started in Aunt Lucy's kitchen," said Tess.

"If they get married, will he be our uncle?" asked Rosie.

The three thought a moment.

"*Yes!*" squealed Tess.

"Oh my goodness!" cried Rosie.

"*Uncle Michael!*" cried Lily.

"Isn't life with Aunt Lucy just wonderful?" said Rosie.

Then the cousins filled a plate with muffins and went out under the shady maple to make plans ... for Aunt Lucy's wedding!

To read about the
Cobble Street Cousins'
next project,
flip the book.

A
LITTLE
SHOPPING

TABLE OF
CONTENTS

For Cousin Karen

C.R.

For Cousins Kale and Alice

W.A.H.

A
LITTLE
SHOPPING

A LITTLE FLOWER SHOP

In a pretty blue house on Cobble Street, three girls named Rosie, Lily, and Tess lived with their Aunt Lucy. Rosie and Lily were sisters and Tess was their cousin, and while the girls' parents—who were dancers with the ballet—were touring the world for a year, the girls were all having a wonderful time staying with Aunt Lucy.

1

When Aunt Lucy went off to her flower shop each morning, the cousins walked together to fourth grade at a sturdy brick school on Olive Street. After school, they walked home and amused themselves while they waited for Aunt Lucy to close the shop and join them.

It was on a sunny afternoon in October as the cousins were playing with Rosie's paper

dolls that Lily had an idea. (Lily was very good with ideas. She wanted to be a writer when she grew up—a poet—so she listened for ideas in her head all the time.)

"I think we need a project," she said.

"What sort of project?" asked Tess, putting a yellow shawl across the shoulders of her doll.

"Well, here we are, all together, looking for things to do every afternoon," said Lily. "So I think we should make something. Something amazing."

Rosie, who was very domestic and loved being at home for any reason at all, said, "That's a great idea. But what?"

Lily leaned in toward the girls with a look of cheerful conspiracy in her eyes.

"Let's make Aunt Lucy a flower shop," she said.

"For goodness sakes, Lily, Aunt Lucy already has a flower shop," said Tess, rolling her eyes dramatically. Tess often rolled her eyes, for she hoped to be on Broadway someday and thought it was good practice.

"No, I mean like a little dollhouse," said Lily. "Except it will be a little flower shop."

"That's a *wonderful* idea," said Rosie. "We can make little pots and tiny flowers."

"And a white picket fence along the front," said Lily.

"We can even make Aunt Lucy," said Tess. "And *Michael*!"

The cousins giggled in delight. Michael and Aunt Lucy were sweethearts, and it was all because the cousins had sold Michael some cookies in the summer and introduced him to Aunt Lucy. Michael was very sweet and kind to the girls, and they all hoped he'd marry Aunt Lucy someday.

"Let's make a list of things we'll need," said Lily. "I'll get my fountain pen."

Lily always used her fountain pen for important writing. She wrote all her poems with it, and letters to her parents, and thoughts in her journal.

She kept her pen and papers under a little wicker bed in the attic. The cousins all had "rooms" of their own in Aunt Lucy's attic. Lily's room, in the middle of the attic, was surrounded by lacy yellow curtains. Rosie's room, on the south end, was behind a lovely old patchwork quilt. And Tess's room, on the north end, was tucked behind a screen decorated with palm trees. Each girl had her own special things in her room, and each respected the others' privacy.

But a large part of the attic was set aside for The Playground, as Lily had named it, and here the cousins spread pillows and blankets, watercolors and brushes, comic books and paperbacks, dolls and stuffed toys, and here they made all their plans.

When Aunt Lucy came home
the girls were still so busy with
their lists and designs that
they almost didn't
want to stop
for tea.

But they
loved having tea
with Aunt Lucy every
afternoon, and not even for a
wonderful idea would they miss it.

The cousins ran downstairs to join her
in the parlor. Aunt Lucy was young and very
pretty. She had long red hair and freckled skin,

and she wore such colorful clothes: bright
pink jumpers, lime green jackets, blouses with
glittery moons and stars. But Aunt Lucy's
house was completely old-fashioned and her
parlor was, as Lily described it, "quaintly
quaint."

The girls sat in white wicker chairs and balanced their teacups and saucers on their laps while Aunt Lucy told them about her day. Elliott—Tess's black and white cat who lived in the attic, too—wandered into the room and rubbed against Aunt Lucy's legs as she talked.

"The sweetest old gentleman came by the shop today," said Aunt Lucy. "He wanted to send his wife something special to celebrate the day they first met, at an ice-cream parlor.

"So I went to French's Market and bought some cones and sprinkles, and I filled each cone with a white carnation. A little glue and chocolate sprinkles, some greenery and bows—it was an ice-cream bouquet!"

"Yum," said Tess. "Makes me want a banana split."

"Where do you buy all the little decorating things you use, Aunt Lucy?" asked Lily, giving Rosie and Tess a "pay attention" look.

"Oh, here and there. But the place I like best is The Olde Craft Shoppe over on Vine."

"Near Michael's apartment?" grinned Rosie.

Aunt Lucy blushed.

"Well, yes, but I liked it best *before* I met him," she said with an embarrassed smile.

"Are the decorating things expensive?" asked Lily, still gathering serious information.

"Oh no," said Aunt Lucy. "There are boxes and boxes of small loose things, old things and new things, and some cost as little as a penny apiece."

Lily and Tess looked at each other and nodded. They knew just where to head tomorrow after school.

"Do you think you'll marry Michael?" Rosie asked Aunt Lucy.

"Oh my goodness!" said Aunt Lucy, all flustered. "Heavens!"

"Is that a yes?" asked Tess.

The cousins giggled and giggled. Then Aunt Lucy smiled and kissed them all and cleared away the tea tray. She was still bright pink as she headed toward the kitchen.

SMALL THINGS

*I*f we're going to the craft shop, we have to stop and see Michael," said Rosie the next day. Of the three cousins, Rosie was the most particularly fond of Michael. She loved sweet, gentle people who smiled at her.

The girls were walking directly from school over to Vine, and each had a book bag across her shoulders.

"Ugh," said Tess. "Of all days, I had to pick

this one to borrow an atlas from the library.
My bag is so heavy."

"Why do you need an atlas?" asked Lily.

"Well, when *I* go on tour someday," said
Tess, "I want to know where I'm going. So I
thought I'd start to get to know the world."

Tess loved to sing, and she felt sure she
would be a performer one day. She collected
old records of all kinds—opera, blues, jazz,

show tunes—and she knew the words to every song she owned. Sometimes, when Lily and Rosie were bored, Tess would sing a number for them.

"I don't want to know the world," said Rosie. "I want to live on Cobble Street forever."

"Well, Mother and Dad definitely won't like that," said Lily. "They want us to travel the globe, like they're doing."

"I'd rather stay home and sew," said Rosie.

Lily and Tess giggled.

"Rosie, you are such a . . . a . . . a *Rosie!*" said Tess.

Rosie grinned. It wasn't such a bad thing to be.

The cousins saw Michael's apartment building, flanked by the two stone lions, just ahead.

"Please, let's just ring and see if he wants company," said Rosie. "With Mrs. Haverstock back in Chicago, he has no one to talk to."

Mrs. Haverstock, Michael's sister, had stayed with him for a while in the summer because Michael had fallen and broken his leg. But now Mrs. Haverstock had returned to her husband and three Scottie dogs in Chicago.

"All right, we can stop," said Lily. "Let's tell him about making the flower shop."

"And about Aunt Lucy saying 'Heavens!' and 'Oh my goodness!'" giggled Tess.

The girls stepped inside the door and rang the bell for Apartment 5.

"Yes?" said Michael's voice.

"Roses are red

Violets are blue

Cousins are here

To see only you," said Lily.

"Good poem, Lily," said Michael. "Hi, girls. Come on in."

Michael buzzed the girls into the hallway and was waiting for them when they reached the door of Apartment 5.

"Are you studying?" asked Rosie. "Are we intruding?"

"Yes, I'm studying and *please* intrude," said Michael, stepping aside. Michael was studying to be a botanist. Anyone could tell that he loved botany, for his living room was filled to overflowing with plants and trees. Michael's family was wealthy—in fact, his father owned the elegant apartment building—but Michael wasn't interested in the family fortune. He wanted simply to be a botanist.

Michael was definitely the perfect match for the young woman who owned Lucy's Flowers. At least, the cousins thought so.

The girls told Michael about their flower shop idea and asked if he'd like to come along to the craft shop.

"Well, I shouldn't," said Michael. "I have a big exam in a couple of days."

"But," he said, smiling at the girls, "I could use an ice-cream cone. Can we make two stops?"

"I can't believe you said that," said Tess. "I've been craving a banana split since yesterday."

"Great," said Michael. "Let's go."

When the cousins and Michael reached the The Olde Craft Shoppe, things were not as they expected.

A tiny wrinkled woman was rushing about on the sidewalk, looking up into the trees and toward the roofs of the buildings.

"Oh no, oh no," she was saying. "Poor Petey, poor little Petey."

"Is anything wrong, ma'am?" asked Michael.

"My parrot escaped," said the woman. "I'm always so careful, but today, I don't know how it happened . . . Petey flew right out the window."

The woman pointed to the small apartment building next to the shop. A curtain fluttered through an open window.

Michael and the girls arched their necks to look as far up into the trees as they could.

"I don't see him," said Michael.

"Neither do I," said Tess.

"Nope," said Lily.

"Is he green and yellow with a fancy head?" asked Rosie.

"*Yes!*" said the tiny woman. "Where is he?"

Rosie pointed to an antiques shop across the street.

"He's on the rooster," she said.

Everyone looked. Sure enough, there was Petey on the rooster weather vane above the antiques shop. There was a slight breeze, and Petey was slowly spinning around and around. He seemed to be having quite a good time.

"Petey!" called the tiny woman. "Petey, you come home right now!"

Petey just ignored her and kept spinning.

Michael looked at the cousins.

"Why don't I walk over there and see if I can help coax Petey down? You girls can do your shopping and meet me when you're finished."

The cousins were very reluctant to leave all the excitement outside, but they knew that Aunt Lucy would be expecting them home in an hour. And there was still ice cream to squeeze in . . . .

"Okay," said Tess. "But come in and get us if something *remarkable* happens."

"I promise," said Michael. He followed the tiny woman across the street, heading for Petey.

The Olde Craft Shoppe was wonderful. There were big tables covered with dozens of little boxes of *everything*.

"It's like a fairyland flea market," said Lily, running her hands through a box of tiny silver stars.

"I love it," said Rosie.

"Me too," said Tess.

And they forgot all about Petey.

It took the cousins about twenty minutes to find everything they needed. If they could have stayed all afternoon, they surely would have.

But, with several little bags of small wonderful things, they finally stepped outside in search of Michael and Petey.

Michael and the tiny woman were still standing under the weather vane, looking up. And Petey was still spinning.

"Petey's having a fun day," said Rosie as the cousins joined Michael.

"Petey!" called the tiny woman. "Petey, you come home right now!"

"Did you get everything you need?" Michael asked the girls.

"Yes, and more," said Lily. "It was wonderful. Miniature teapots and tiny wheelbarrows and the sweetest little wicker chairs."

"I bought some glitter," said Tess. "I'm going to scatter it in my hair for my next performance."

"And I bought some beautiful silver thread, to repair my bear, Henry," said Rosie, digging into one of her bags. "See?"

She held out a silvery spool for Michael to see.

And just then...*flappa-flappa-flappa-PECK!* Petey flew down and with his beak plucked the spool of thread right out of Rosie's hand!

"Eeek!" squealed Rosie.

"Hey!" yelled Tess.

"Petey!" scolded the tiny woman.

They all watched as Petey
circled above their heads with his
wonderful prize. And then, slowly
and rather casually, he turned and
flew right back into his apartment.

"Yay!" clapped the cousins.

"Oh thank goodness," said the tiny woman.

"You'd better run right in and close that
window," said Michael.

"Oh yes, oh yes," the tiny woman said, hurrying away. "Little girl, I'll buy you another spool of thread."

"That's all right," called Michael. "No need! Happy to help!"

He turned to Rosie.

"Let's buy another spool, Rosie," he said. "I'll pay for it."

Rosie smiled.

"I'd rather you pay for a chocolate fudge cone with sprinkles."

Michael laughed.

"*Double* sprinkles," he said. "Maybe even triple."

Rosie took Michael's hand, and everyone walked happily to the ice cream parlor, talking, of course, of nothing but Petey.

SURPRISE!

Lily, Rosie, and Tess worked secretly on Aunt Lucy's flower shop for several days. First they cut pieces of cardboard and glued them into the shape of the building. Then they gave the cardboard two thick coats of white paint. Finally they began the fun part: decorating.

38

Because they hadn't any color photographs of Aunt Lucy's *real* flower shop, the cousins sometimes forgot exactly what it looked like.

When this happened—and it was daytime—
one of the girls would dash down to the corner
and take a good look at the shop. (Was the
bench on the right or left side of the door?)
Then she would run home with the information and the girls would begin again.

As they worked on the little shop, the cousins talked of all sorts of things. Whom they most admired, which books they liked best, where they wanted to take a vacation. And, as always, they talked of what they wanted to be.

"All of this making things on a budget is good for me," said Lily. "Because poets are

always poor. They live in tiny apartments above movie houses or cafés. And their friends all worry about them and bring them food. When I'm a poet, I'll have some practice making do."

"Well," said Tess, "I definitely do *not* want to be poor and this 'making do' is a good reminder for me. It reminds me that when I'm a Broadway star, I want to be *loaded*." She gave a mischievous grin.

The girls worked quietly a moment. Then Lily asked, "What about you, Rosie?"

Rosie looked up from the tiny chimney she was intently gluing on.

"Oh," she said, "this reminds *me* that I like to play with glue."

Lily and Tess giggled and giggled. Rosie said the most sensible things, but they always came out funny.

Finally by Saturday the flower shop was finished and the girls invited Michael over to share in their surprise. When Aunt Lucy arrived home from shopping, all four were sitting on the front porch.

"Michael!" exclaimed Aunt Lucy. "It's so nice to see you!" Aunt Lucy was looking very pretty. Her long red hair was in a ponytail, and she wore big silver hoop earrings.

The cousins could see that Michael really liked Aunt Lucy. He always turned so pink and clumsy when she showed up.

Michael reached out to help with Aunt Lucy's bags and nearly dropped them. The cousins looked at each other and smiled.

"The girls tell me they have a surprise for you," said Michael, holding the bags and the door open for Aunt Lucy. "I haven't seen it. I just hope its name isn't Petey."

Rosie giggled.

"At least I'd get my spool of thread back," she said.

Once the bags were put away and Aunt Lucy and Michael were settled on the front porch swing, the cousins had Aunt Lucy hide her eyes as they carried out the little flower shop. Then she looked.

"Oh my gracious!" she said. "It's my flower shop! Oh my goodness!"

The shop was glued to a flat board. Aunt Lucy picked it up and turned it around and around.

"Oh, you sweet girls," she said. "It's *beautiful!*"

And it was. It had the blue-painted window boxes and bold yellow door of Aunt Lucy's shop. It had the green park bench in front and the wishing well by the gate. It had windows that said LUCY'S FLOWERS and a little sign that said OPEN. And—best of all—it had Aunt Lucy! There she was, a little wooden doll with long red yarn for hair and a polka-dot dress.

Michael smiled at Aunt Lucy.

"It looks just like you," he said. "And I mean that in a good way."

"We have one more little surprise," said Tess.

She pulled something from her pocket.

A Michael doll!

"Yikes," said Michael.

The doll had Michael's messy hair and baggy sport coat—and in its hand was a tiny book that said *Botany*.

"Does my hair really look like that?" asked Michael.

"Yes," said Lily. "And I mean that in a good way."

Everybody laughed.

"Now if you get lonely, Aunt Lucy," said Rosie, "you can have Michael visit you." Rosie walked the Michael doll up to the shop door.

"Hmmm," said Aunt Lucy. "Too bad he doesn't have a box of chocolates in his *other* hand!"

"Oops. Guess we'll just have to make a trip back to The Olde Craft Shoppe," Tess said, grinning.

"Actually, I would love to go back there," said Lily. "There were some pretty lace doilies I could write poems on."

"And I could get more thread," said Rosie. "Henry Bear's arm is still loose."

"I'd like some big feathers," said Tess. "For my next performance."

"Why don't we all go?" said Michael. "And I'll spring for ice cream on the way home."

"Great!" said the girls.

So everyone walked over to Vine Street and The Olde Craft Shoppe. This time Petey wasn't riding on the rooster, so the street was very peaceful and the girls were able to browse in the shop for a long time. Michael was very patient. He occupied himself with a box of miniature trains while everyone explored.

Then, after stopping for ice cream as promised, they all walked back to Michael's apartment for tea. Michael loved exotic teas, so the cousins always had to try something new and strange, like Ginger Licorice Mint or Maple Tangerine. But the girls liked Michael so much that they didn't mind. And he always let them sit on his dragon bench with their teacups.

When the cousins and Aunt Lucy finally returned home, everyone was so tired. They all wanted a nap. Aunt Lucy hugged each girl tight and thanked them all again for being such sweet angels. Then the cousins went up to the attic and snuggled into their own beds.

Behind the long, lacy yellow curtains, Lily said, "Tomorrow I'll write everyone a little poem on a doily."

"And I," called Tess, "will make us some crazy hats with big feathers."

Things were quiet.

Then Rosie said, "Let me know if anyone needs an arm sewn back on."

Lily and Tess giggled and giggled.

"I meant your *toys*," called Rosie.

And everyone went to sleep with a smile.

THE • COBBLE • STREET • COUSINS

SPECIAL
GIFTS

CYNTHIA RYLANT

illustrated by

WENDY ANDERSON HALPERIN

ALADDIN PAPERBACKS
New York London Toronto Sydney Singapore

For Cousin Stephanie

C.R.

For my very special cousin Zoe

W.A.H.

WINTER VACATION

Lily, Rosie, and Tess—all nine years old—
lived with their Aunt Lucy in a lovely
blue house on Cobble Street. Lily and Rosie
were sisters, Tess was their cousin, and Aunt
Lucy was aunt to everyone. The girls'
parents all danced with the ballet,
and while the ballet toured the
world for a year, the cousins
were sharing Aunt Lucy's attic.

1

It was wonderful. Each girl had her own
little nook in the attic: Lily's bed was behind
the long, lacy yellow curtains; Rosie's bed was
behind the old patchwork quilt; and Tess's bed

was behind the screen decorated with palm trees. The girls loved their special places, and when they all wanted to be together, they came out into The Playground—a big pile of blankets and books and toys in the middle of the room.

It was in The Playground where they began discussing Winter Vacation. Soon school would be out for three weeks. What would they do for fun?

"I suggest we learn to ice-skate," said Tess, stroking her cat, Elliott, in her arms. Tess wanted to sing on Broadway someday, and she looked for any opportunity to perform—even if it meant performing falls on ice.

"Oh no," said Rosie. "I couldn't. I'm clumsy, I'm shy, and I hate cold fingers." (Rosie loved most being quiet and warm and at home.)

"You're not clumsy," said Lily. "But you're right, Rosie, you do hate cold fingers. And I, for one, hate a sore bottom, which is exactly what I'd have if I tried to ice-skate."

"You girls are *so* unadventurous!" said Tess.

"Pain does not equal adventure," said Lily.

"Well then, what ideas do you have?" asked Tess.

"Hmmm," said Lily, who loved ideas and coming up with them. (She hoped to be a writer someday.) "Maybe we could learn to do something less cold and painful. How about sewing?"

"I'd love to learn to sew!" exclaimed Rosie.

"Ugh," said Tess. "Boring."

"If you learn to sew, Tess," said Lily, "you can make your own costumes. You can make capes and skirts and—"

"You're right!" said Tess. "But where do we learn to sew?"

"At Mrs. White's house, of course," said Lily.

"Of course!" said Rosie and Tess.

Mrs. White was a very elderly woman the cousins had met in the summer when they delivered cookies to her on her ninetieth birthday. Since then, she had become their friend and they often stopped in to see her and chat. And whenever they visited, Mrs. White gave each of them a little cat she had sewn herself.

"I'd love to make some cotton dolls with dresses," said Rosie.

"I'd love to make a vest—with sequins," said Tess.

"I could make little pillows and decorate them with words," said Lily. "Like 'WISH.'"

"'WISH'?" said Tess. "That's all?"

"That's *everything*!" said Lily.

"What could we do for Mrs. White in return?" asked Rosie.

"I don't know," said Lily. "Let's ask her."

"And we have to ask Aunt Lucy," reminded Tess.

"Oh, Aunt Lucy will love the idea," said Lily. "She loves everything."

It did seem that Aunt Lucy loved everything. She certainly loved having the three girls live with her in her big, old-fashioned house. Aunt Lucy was young and pretty. She had long red hair and freckles and she wore the most wonderful clothes—jumpers covered with sunflowers, perky antique hats, shiny yellow lace-up boots. She owned a flower shop on the corner—Lucy's Flowers—and the cousins loved to visit her there. They drank tea and talked with the customers.

Their favorite customer, of course, was Michael Livingston, Lucy's boyfriend. The cousins had met Michael first and had introduced him to Aunt Lucy, and they were quite proud of their match-making. Michael lived nearby in an elegant apartment building owned by his wealthy family, and he was studying to be a botanist. The cousins all looked forward to the day he and Aunt Lucy would marry.

"Let's go to the flower shop and tell Aunt Lucy of our idea right now," said Rosie.

"We'll tell her we'll sew something just for her," said Lily.

"Like a *wedding* dress!" said Tess.

Giggling with excitement, the cousins bounded down the attic steps and went to find Aunt Lucy.